Old Sticky

Michael Morpurgo

Illustrated by Frances Thatcher

Old Sticky stood right in the middle of Market Square which was right in the middle of town. They called her Old Sticky because she was a chestnut tree and her buds were always sticky in the spring; but she wasn't just any old chestnut tree. She was the last chestnut tree in town. Indeed, she was the last *tree* in town. All the rest had been cut down to make way for houses and roads and shops and factories and car parks.

So when she rustled in the breeze, she rustled alone, and when she whistled in the wind, she whistled alone, and when she roared in a gale, she roared alone.

For the children in the town, Old
Sticky was all the playground they
could want. They could swing on her
branches and play with her conkers.
They could build their treehouses in
her and, in the autumn, they could
bury each other in golden piles of her
fallen leaves.

Of course everyone in town had been a child at one time or another, and so everyone loved Old Sticky (everyone, that is, except Mr Humpage, the road sweeper, who had to sweep up her leaves).

Old Sticky had been there longer than the Town Hall itself, longer than the school. Some people even said that Old Sticky was so old, the town must have been built around her.

There was one person in the town, however, who knew and loved Old Sticky more than anyone else. Tully lived high up in the top flat of a house on the north side of the Square. Ever since he could remember, Old Sticky had knocked on his window to wake him up in the mornings. He had only to open his window to touch her—she was that close. When measles and mumps and chicken-pox and ear-ache kept him in bed, he would spend all day gazing out of the window at the busy woodpeckers or the squabbling jackdaws.

At night, with the owl hooting outside his window, he would look up at the ceiling of his bedroom and watch the changing patterns made by Old Sticky's shadow as she swayed her branches in the moonlight. It helped him to go off to sleep.

7

But there was someone else in town who liked Old Sticky almost as much as Tully. Percival Pinkerton liked Old Sticky so much that he wanted to cut her down and make her into cupboards and tables and chairs. It was the same Mr Pinkerton who had cut down every other tree in town, and it was the same Mr Pinkerton who owned the timber-yard down by the railway station.

What's more, Percival Pinkerton was the mayor, and that meant that, by and large, most people did what he said. Even so, he knew that everyone in town loved Old Sticky so much that he would have to find a very good excuse if he wanted to cut her down.

Then, one stormy November night, while Tully was still fast asleep, one of Old Sticky's branches broke and came crashing down into the Square, flattening the wooden seat below where the townspeople would come to sit and talk on summer evenings.

Percival Pinkerton's chance had come.

Mr Pinkerton was there first thing in the morning. So was Mr Humpage, the road sweeper; so was Tully and so was half the town.

"Well, well, well," said Mr Pinkerton, trying to look sad. "It's a crying shame, of course, but all good things have to come to an end. I'm afraid she's too dangerous. We'll have to cut her down."

"But you can't!" the townspeople cried. "You can't cut down Old Sticky!"

Percival Pinkerton had a wicked way with words, and he knew it. It would be easy enough to persuade them, particularly Mrs Maplethorpe, the vicar's wife. She spent more time sitting and talking on the bench than anyone else.

"Now, just supposing," he said, "just supposing, Mrs Maplethorpe, that you yourself had been sitting there on the bench last night, and that great big branch had come crashing down on top of you."

Mrs Maplethorpe had not thought of it quite that way, not until now. "Well, perhaps Mr Pinkerton's right after all," she said. "I mean if I had been sitting there last night … can you imagine? Dear me, it makes me shiver just to think about it!"

"But she wasn't sitting there last night," thought Tully.

"And what if it had come down on market day," said Mr Pinkerton, "with the Square full of stalls and barrows and crowds of men, women and little children?"

"But it didn't happen on market day," thought Tully. "It happened on a dark, stormy night when no one was about."

"And what if the children had been playing under the tree when the branch came down?" said Mr Pinkerton. "What then?" And everyone had to agree that would have been a terrible thing, except Tully.

"But we weren't," said Tully out loud, before he could stop himself. "We were all in bed, weren't we?"

Percival Pinkerton cast a mean look at Tully. "That tree is dangerous," he said. "What happened once can happen again. She's got to come down."

And although it made them sad and they didn't like the idea one bit, most people thought he was right, but not the children.

"About time too," said Mr Humpage. "Better off without trees if you ask me. Trees have leaves and leaves fall off and it's me that has to sweep 'em up day after day. Down with her, that's what I say."

"But you can't," cried Tully. "You can't cut Old Sticky down just because a branch broke off. It's not her fault there was a storm last night."

"Now listen here, Tully," said Mr
Pinkerton, who did not care to be
argued with. "Everyone agrees that the
tree is dangerous. I'm the mayor of this
town and I'm telling you that this tree
has to be cut down and right now.
Why, the next time, the whole tree
could come down."

And everyone agreed that that was
true, except for the children.

"But where are we going to play if you cut Old Sticky down?" they cried.

"Where are we going to swing? Where are we going to climb? Where are we going to build our treehouses?"

"And where are the birds going to sing?" asked Tully.

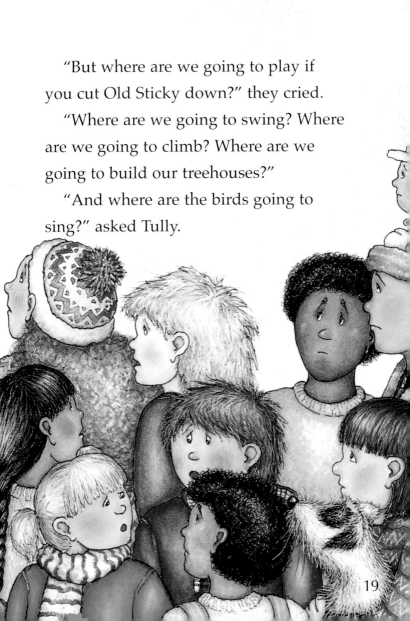

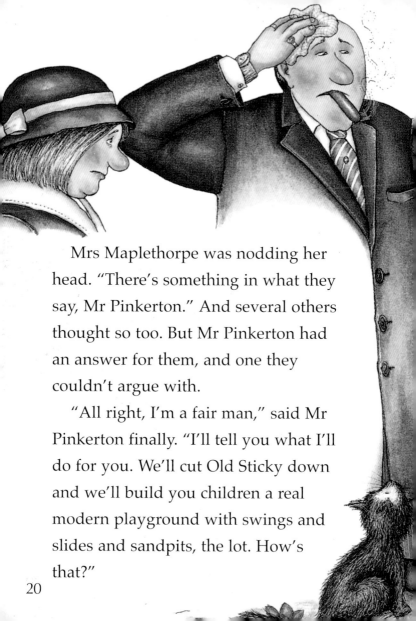

Mrs Maplethorpe was nodding her head. "There's something in what they say, Mr Pinkerton." And several others thought so too. But Mr Pinkerton had an answer for them, and one they couldn't argue with.

"All right, I'm a fair man," said Mr Pinkerton finally. "I'll tell you what I'll do for you. We'll cut Old Sticky down and we'll build you children a real modern playground with swings and slides and sandpits, the lot. How's that?"

A few of the children thought that was a fine idea, but most of them did not.

"Where are we going to get our conkers from?" they said.

"And where are the birds going to sing?" asked Tully again.

But in spite of everything they said, it was decided there and then that Old Sticky had to be cut down, and right away.

Up came the men from the timber-yard with their saws and ladders and ropes. They measured out how high Old Sticky was and tied ropes to her branches. They worked out where she would fall and marked off a danger area. They put on their yellow helmets and sharpened their saws.

Everyone was so busy that they never noticed Tully and his friends as they linked arms and made a chain of children around Old Sticky.

"We're ready to cut her down," Mr Pinkerton shouted, and he blew his whistle. "Stand back! Stand back!"

But Tully and his friends would not move.

"Old Sticky stays!" they chanted. "Old Sticky stays!"

"We're not moving, Mr Pinkerton," said Tully. "If we stay here, you can't cut Old Sticky down. And we're not moving."

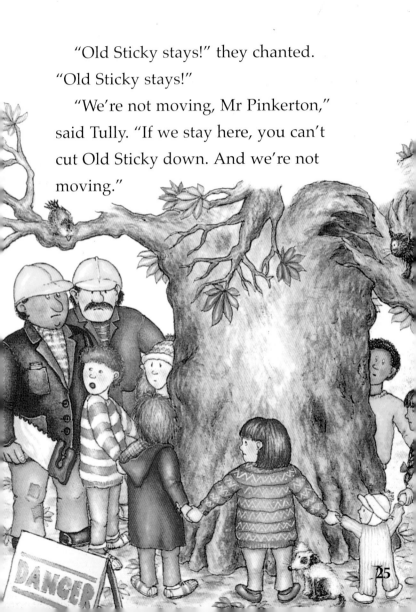

First their mothers came, then their fathers and then Mrs Maplethorpe, the vicar's wife. They all tried to persuade the children to move, but the children would not budge. Even sweets and toffee apples would not tempt them away. They begged and pleaded, but still the children would not move.

By now Percival Pinkerton had had quite enough. "Very well children," he said, "if you won't come away on your own, then we shall have to move you ourselves. You have five minutes to make up your mind."

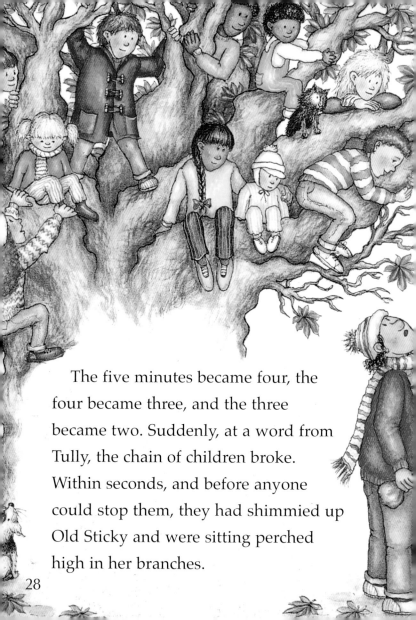

The five minutes became four, the
four became three, and the three
became two. Suddenly, at a word from
Tully, the chain of children broke.
Within seconds, and before anyone
could stop them, they had shimmied up
Old Sticky and were sitting perched
high in her branches.

28

"Now listen here," roared Percival Pinkerton, purple in the face. "If you don't come down this instant, I'll … I'll …"

"Come down! Come down!" cried the townspeople. "What if another branch breaks and you fall? What if the wind blows you down? Oh, please come down, please!"

"We'll come down," Tully called back, "but only if you take away the saws and ladders and ropes and leave Old Sticky be. Old Sticky stays!"

And all the children chanted, "Old Sticky stays! Old Sticky stays!"

The wind blew and the branches shook and the people screamed below. But still the children would not come down.

Down below in Market Square, Mr Pinkerton was surrounded by angry mothers and fathers. "All right, all right," he said at last. "I'll get your children down, just leave it to me."

He walked across the Square and
whispered to the men from the timber-
yard. Then he called up to the children.
"You can come down, children.
We're putting away the saws and
ladders and ropes just like you wanted.
Look."

And sure enough, they were, but there was a nasty look in Percival Pinkerton's eye that the children could not see.

Up in Old Sticky the children cheered and cheered and cheered; and then, one by one, they climbed down.

Last of all came Tully, who was rushed home to a hot bath and a cup of steaming hot chocolate.

He had almost finished his hot chocolate when he heard Old Sticky banging on his window, banging so hard that he thought the window might break. Tully looked out.

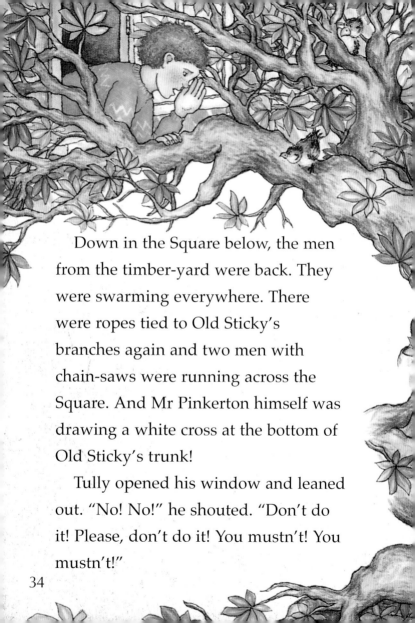

Down in the Square below, the men from the timber-yard were back. They were swarming everywhere. There were ropes tied to Old Sticky's branches again and two men with chain-saws were running across the Square. And Mr Pinkerton himself was drawing a white cross at the bottom of Old Sticky's trunk!

Tully opened his window and leaned out. "No! No!" he shouted. "Don't do it! Please, don't do it! You mustn't! You mustn't!"

Everyone in the Square looked up, and what they saw made their hearts stop. Tully was clambering out onto his window ledge.

Down in the Square, they held their
breath as Tully jumped across into Old
Sticky. He caught hold of a branch and
swung himself higher up the tree.
"You can't cut her down now," he called
out. "And I'm not coming down, not till
you promise you won't cut Old Sticky
down. And this time you must promise
out loud, so that everyone can hear you."

Everyone turned to look at Mr Pinkerton, and he knew he had no choice. "All right, Tully. I promise," he said. "I promise I won't cut Old Sticky down."

"You promise? You promise truthfully?" said Tully, who wanted to be quite sure this time.

"I promise, I promise truthfully," said Mr Pinkerton. "Cross my heart."

But at that moment a sudden wind blew in from nowhere, and Old Sticky began to whistle and roar. Before he knew it, Tully had been shaken off his branch and was hanging on by his fingers, clinging for dear life.

Down in Market Square, the crowd gasped. Percy Pinkerton (who was not all bad) ran to call the fire brigade, and soon Tully heard the whine of the sirens as the fire engines came racing up the hill. The Square filled with people, all looking up and hoping and praying Tully would not fall. Tully felt his fingers slipping, but he held on.

"Hang on!" everyone cried. "Hang on! We'll soon have you down."

So the firemen ran up their longest ladder, but it was not long enough. They tried climbing up into the tree, but they could not reach him. Tully could feel his fingers slipping further and further.

"I can't hang on any longer," Tully thought. "I'm going to fall! Oh, help me, Old Sticky. Please, help me!"

Quite suddenly the wind dropped
and Old Sticky was still. Then she
seemed to shiver and sigh, as if she
were taking a deep breath.

Slowly the branch began to bend.
"Oh no, it's going to break," Tully
thought. But it didn't. It bent and it
bent until Tully found himself standing
on the branch below. He knew then
that Old Sticky was helping him down!

The townspeople looked on as Tully climbed down from branch to branch until his feet touched the ground and he was safe. Everyone clapped and cheered and Mrs Maplethorpe cried.

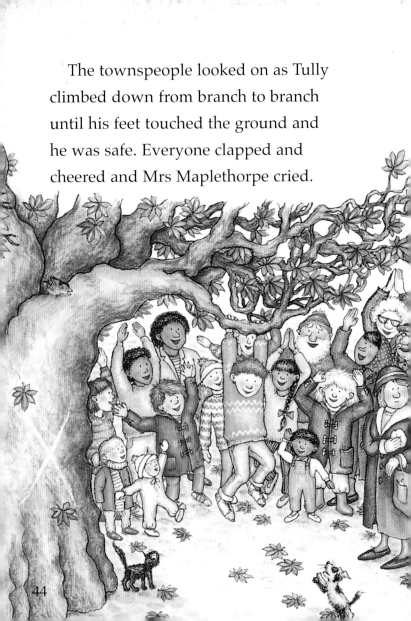

Someone put a fireman's helmet on
Tully's head and he was carried in
tumultuous triumph around the Square.
Even Mr Humpage was seen dancing
around his broom in wild delight.

45

Someone said it was the wind that moved the branches and helped Tully down, but Tully knew it wasn't and so did Percival Pinkerton.

"And to think," said Mr Pinkerton, "to think I was going to cut that tree down and make cupboards and tables and chairs out of her."

"But what about our wooden seat?" asked Mrs Maplethorpe. "Where is everyone going to sit and talk on summer evenings?"

"We'll just have to make you another one," said Mr Pinkerton. "Perhaps we could make it out of the branch that blew off Old Sticky last night—if that's all right with Old Sticky, of course."

"You'd better ask her," said Tully.

Percival Pinkerton looked up at Old Sticky and asked her, and Old Sticky shivered her branches and bowed her head in reply.

"I think she's saying 'yes'," said Tully.